W9-AYC-724

Withdrawn

The Very Little
Princess

The Very Little
Princess

by Marion Dane Bauer

illustrated by Elizabeth Sayles

Random House 🏠 New York

For Barbara Ann Hill
—M.D.B.

Text copyright © 2010 by Marion Dane Bauer
Illustrations copyright © 2010 by Elizabeth Sayles

Visit us on the Web!
www.steppingstonesbooks.com
www.randomhouse.com/kids

Educators and librarians, for a variety of teaching tools, visit us at
www.randomhouse.com/teachers

Library of Congress Cataloging-in-Publication Data
Bauer, Marion Dane.
The very little princess / by Marion Dane Bauer ; illustrated by Elizabeth Sayles.
— 1st ed.
    p.   cm.
"A Stepping Stone Book."
Summary: When she goes to her grandmother's house for the first time, Zoey finds a tiny china doll that comes alive in her hands and believes that she is a princess and that Zoey is her servant.
ISBN 978-0-375-85691-4 (trade) — ISBN 978-0-375-95691-1 (lib. bdg.) —
ISBN 978-0-375-85693-8 (pbk.)
[1. Dolls—Fiction. 2. Mothers and daughters—Fiction. 3. Grandmothers—Fiction.]
I. Sayles, Elizabeth, ill. II. Title.
PZ7.B3262Ve 2009
[Fic]—dc22   2009005039

Printed in the United States of America
10 9 8 7 6 5 4 3 2 1
First Edition

Contents

Chapter 1

A Girl and a Doll

This is a story about a girl and a doll. A brave girl and a . . . well, a doll is just a doll, isn't she? Or at least that's all she was when this story began.

The doll was made of fine china, and she was very small. She was, in fact, exactly three and one-quarter inches tall from head to toe. Her eyes were blue, and her hair was spun gold. Or if you feel less romantic about hair, you could say it was straw yellow.

The girl saw spun gold.

The girl's name was Zoey, and the doll hadn't always been hers. In fact, it had once belonged to a grandmother so far removed that no one seemed to have any idea how many *greats* it would take to name her.

But Zoey didn't yet know about the doll the morning her mother told her it was time to get ready to go.

"Go where?" she asked.

"To your grandmother's house," her mother replied. And she smiled as though going off to Zoey's grandmother's house on a June morning were the most natural thing in the world.

Of course, visiting your grandmother probably is natural for you. But it wasn't for Zoey. The truth is she had never met her grandmother. Until that moment she hadn't even known she *had* a grandmother!

"Go *where*?" Zoey asked again, amazed.

"To your grandmother's house," Zoey's mother repeated. And then she picked Zoey up and twirled her around so that her feet came off the floor and flew through the air.

Zoey was almost too big to be twirled around that way, but her mother still did it from time to time. Only when she was in a very good mood, though. Zoey was glad her mother was in a good mood. She'd been awfully quiet lately.

"Now go pack," her mom said when she put Zoey down.

So Zoey did. She got out her pink cardboard ballerina suitcase and put in shorts and shirts and underpants and pajamas. Then she added a sweatshirt, just in case it was cold where her grandmother lived.

She put in her hairbrush, too, the one that didn't tangle in her too-curly hair, and a toothbrush.

And because her mother hadn't said how long they would be staying, she put in the book her teacher had given her for being the best reader in the fourth grade. She had read it already, but a good book can be read many times.

While she packed, Zoey thought about her grandmother. The idea that she had a real grandmother thrilled her!

As far as Zoey had ever known, she had no family except her mother. No grandparents. No aunts. No uncles. No cousins. No brothers or sisters. No father, either. She and her mother had always been a family of two.

"Two is a just-right number," Zoey's mother often said.

And even when Zoey was very small, she'd said it, too. "A just-right number."

Two meant someone to break wishbones with. It meant someone to sit in front of their tiny TV with, eating popcorn dripping with butter and washed down with cocoa. It meant someone to play endless games of double solitaire with . . . and checkers and Scrabble. Zoey had won their last two games of Scrabble.

Two meant someone to go to when you had a bad dream. Sometimes the bad dream was Zoey's. Sometimes it was her mother's. But always the other was there.

"You and me," Zoey's mom would say, giving Zoey a fierce hug. "We're just right."

And Zoey had always agreed.

But three could be a just-right number, too. Zoey was sure it could. Especially when the third person was her grandmother.

Maybe her grandmother liked to play Scrabble!

Zoey came out of her bedroom with her suitcase, and her mother handed her a piece of peanut butter toast and led the way out of their apartment. Before Zoey had swallowed her last bite of toast, they were driving away.

To her grandmother's house.

They drove out of Minneapolis and into the

countryside. They drove on whizzing four-lane highways and on quiet two-lane ones. They drove and drove and never stopped, except once for gas.

At first Zoey's mother chattered: About the town she'd grown up in . . . so small, she said, they rolled the sidewalks up at night. (Zoey thought about that for a long time, sidewalks rolled up like rugs to leave room for dancing.) About the house she'd grown up in . . . bigger than any apartment Zoey had ever seen. About the room she'd grown up in . . . "Pink enough even for you, Zoey!" her mother added.

But as the ribbon of road unwound and unwound, her mom gradually unwound, too, until finally she went still. After her mother went still, Zoey couldn't think of anything to say about the town and the house and the room and the grandmother she had never seen, so she was still, too. And for the rest of the way, they

drove in silence, except for the sounds Zoey's tummy began to make when lunchtime came and went and they didn't stop. (Sometimes, she knew, her mom just didn't get hungry.)

Zoey quit looking for signs of a Pizza Hut or McDonald's when they turned onto a gravel road.

Theirs was the only car on the gravel road, and the dust billowed behind them like smoke.

When Zoey looked back, she wondered, just for a moment, if the world she knew—their apartment, her school, her friends, all of it— was burning away in that smoke.

But then she told herself she was being foolish.

Finally a small town came into view, and they drove through it slowly. The street and the grocery store and the corner café and the white church with a stubby steeple were quiet, just as quiet as the inside of the car. And when her mom stopped in front of a tall yellow house surrounded by a grassy yard, the house looked quiet, too.

Lilacs grew along the edges of the yard, but the few blossoms remaining had gone papery and brown. Zoey had lived all her life in one apartment or another, though she had often dreamed of a house surrounded by lilacs. In her dream, however, the blooms were fresh and sweet.

Zoey and her mother stepped out of the car and into the sunny afternoon. It smelled of grass and of something else Zoey couldn't name, something she didn't smell in the city. Perhaps it was the earth itself. Whatever it was, it smelled good.

Zoey's mother put a hand in the middle of

Zoey's back and pressed her along the stone walk and up the porch steps. A wicker rocking chair sat alone on the porch. Zoey looked for a swing, but there was none. That was something else she had always dreamed of . . . a porch with a swing.

"Knock," her mother said gently when they'd stepped up onto the porch. Zoey wondered why her mother didn't do it herself, but she lifted her hand to obey.

Before her knuckles even touched the wood, though, the door swung open.

And there stood a woman she had never seen before. Not even in a picture. But Zoey knew instantly who she was. This had to be her very own grandmother.

Chapter 2

A Single Tear

The woman looked like Zoey's mother and not like Zoey's mother at the same time. She had the same dark, fiercely curled hair, though hers was touched with gray. She even had the same freckles. But while Zoey's mother was all flat planes and sharp corners, her grandmother was round and pillowy.

"You must be Zoey." The name came out soft, despite the buzz of the Z. Zoey's grandmother said it as though she liked the shape of Zoey's name in her mouth.

"Hello . . ." Zoey stopped. Should she call her Granny? That's what her best friend, Molly, called *her* grandmother. "I guess I don't know what to call you," Zoey admitted.

"I don't know, either," her grandmother said. She looked past Zoey to her mother as she spoke, and her gaze sharpened. "Since your mother has never thought it worthwhile to bring you to see me until now, maybe you should just call me Hazel."

"Now, Mother," Zoey's mom scolded in a low voice. "Don't be like that."

Zoey looked from her grandmother to her mother, then back to her grandmother again. Clearly there was something going on between the two that she didn't understand.

When Hazel's gaze returned to Zoey, her expression softened once more. "Are you hungry, Zoey?" she asked.

Zoey's stomach had been rumbling for a couple of hours, but she answered politely, "Not really. Thanks." Then she added, because she sensed it was important that Hazel know her mother took good care of her, "My mom made me peanut butter toast this morning."

"Peanut butter toast! This morning!" Hazel

repeated. She clapped her hands to her plump cheeks, turned sharply, and marched away. "Please, come in," she called back over her shoulder just before she disappeared from view. "I'll get you some lunch."

Zoey's mom rolled her eyes as though this were the last thing she wanted . . . to be invited in for lunch. But she handed Zoey the pink suitcase she had brought from the car and, without a word, followed Hazel into the house.

Zoey didn't move. The strange mixture of welcome and accusation in the air seemed to glue her feet to the porch floor.

She *was* hungry, though. Starved, in fact. And Hazel had mentioned lunch.

So Zoey started after them. Before she had gone more than a dozen steps, the argument that had been hanging in the air since the moment the door opened had begun.

"Why?" her grandmother was saying. And, "Do you know . . . ?" And, "It's been more than ten years! I've been so . . ."

Zoey's mother answered. Zoey could tell she was answering, because Hazel went quiet while she did, but Zoey couldn't hear what her mother was saying.

Then her grandmother would come in again, her voice high and bruised-sounding. "You never . . . !"

Zoey stood perfectly still. She wasn't used to arguments. She didn't even argue with her friends very often. And she never argued with her mother!

Her new grandmother had seemed nice when she'd first come to the door. But she didn't seem nice when she talked this way.

Besides, Hazel was a witch's name, wasn't it?

In any case, Zoey wasn't going to walk into

the middle of the argument. She could tell—
without even hearing her name—that it was
about her.

Zoey considered going back outside to the
car, but she'd been riding too long to want to
be there again. She looked around for some-
place else to go, away from the voices. When
she noticed stairs, that seemed as good a solution as any. She'd see where they went.

She climbed the stairs slowly, her cardboard
suitcase banging against her leg. With each step,
the angry voices grew farther away.

In the hallway at the top, Zoey hesitated
for a moment. Perhaps she should go back
downstairs. After all, she hadn't been given
permission to explore.

But then the voices rose to a pitch that she
could hear again, and she started down the
hall, glancing into the rooms on either side.

It should be easy to find her mother's room. It would be pink.

Not this one. Not that one.

The hall ended in front of a closed door. Zoey turned the knob and swung the door open.

"This one!" she breathed. "This is the one!"

It had to be the room her mother had talked about. It was as pink as any she had ever seen.

And white.

And gold.

The walls were papered in pink rosebuds on a creamy white background. The bedspread and the curtains were pink. The furniture was white with gold trim. There was a white and gold dresser and a white and gold dressing table with an oval mirror. The bed had a delicate white and gold post at each corner holding up a ruffled pink canopy.

Across the room was a bay window with a

window seat. And in the middle of the window seat stood a tall object, covered by a sheet.

Zoey set down her suitcase and tiptoed to the window. She touched the sheet. Whatever was hidden under it must be precious. Nothing else in the room was covered this way.

Did she dare peek?

She stepped back, away from temptation, and stuffed her hands into her pockets. This was her grandmother's house. She didn't even know her grandmother. All she knew about Hazel, actually, was that she could be angry.

But, as if they had a will of their own, Zoey's hands crept out of her pockets and reached for the sheet again. This time she let her hands give the sheet a tug. It fell away.

Before her was the most perfect dollhouse she had ever seen!

Zoey released the breath she didn't even

know she'd been holding. Then she knelt before the little house and peered in.

Every room was perfect. The kitchen had a sink and stove. The door of the tiny stove opened and closed. The living room was furnished with a red velvet chair and a red velvet sofa with teensy purple pillows. There was even a footstool in front of the chair for resting the smallest of feet. The bathroom had a toilet, a bathtub, and a sink.

But best of all was the bedroom. It was pink and white, an exact copy of the larger bedroom Zoey was in. The same wallpaper with pink rosebuds. The same white furniture with gold trim. The same dressing table with an oval mirror, and the same canopied bed and window seat.

The only thing missing in the dollhouse bedroom was another, smaller dollhouse.

There was something here, though, that wasn't in the big bedroom. A tiny pink and white doll lay on the ruffled canopied bed!

Zoey picked the doll up, cupping it in the palm of her hand. It was made out of china!

She leaned close to study the perfect china "skin," the gauzy pink gown, the golden hair. And as she did, a single tear that she hadn't even known was there landed—*plop!*—on the doll's face.

Zoey didn't have any idea what had prompted the tear. Was she sad? Frightened? Or maybe it was a tear of pure joy.

Before she could wipe the wet away from the doll's face, though, something happened. It was something so incredible that Zoey would dream this moment, again and again, for the rest of her life and wake each time with her heart pounding.

The tiny doll pushed herself upright in Zoey's hand and sneezed!

Chapter 3

Two Choices

Now, I want you to stop for a moment to think. What would you do if a doll, a tiny china doll lying stiff and still in your hand, sat up suddenly and sneezed?

Would you say, *Oh my! How wonderful! My doll just woke up!*

Or would you toss the thing across the room?

I mean, really.

Having a doll come awake in your hands is a little like having a mouse run across your toes when you are sitting in the bathroom. It isn't that you are afraid of mice exactly. But the suddenness—the unexpectedness—of a live mouse would probably make you jump.

That was Zoey's first reaction. She jumped. And she started to shake her hand to flick the doll away. But something stopped her. Maybe it was the part of her that had always dreamed such a moment as this. Still, her hand definitely wanted to get rid of this strange thing. So she dropped it instead. She let the doll fall, almost gently, onto the floor of the dollhouse.

But now let's imagine something else. This is something that will, perhaps, take a bit more imagining.

Imagine being a doll yourself, a tiny doll, made out of fine china. You've been asleep for years, decades. Or not exactly asleep, since your stillness has been without dreams. But it's been a very long time since you have known

anything or felt anything. And suddenly you find yourself . . .

Awake.

Aware.

Wet.

Lying on the floor in the middle of the doll-house bedroom.

You are thoroughly jolted, fortunately not broken. (If the doll were broken, this story would end much too soon.)

But you can remember just enough to know that you aren't supposed to be on the floor. Didn't you lie down on the soft little bed before you went to sleep?

You are also aware of a lot of freckles.

A nose, too. A pert, turned-up one. It's the kind adults refer to as "cute as a button." But when viewed from below by a very tiny creature, such a nose is not at all appealing. It is gaping and moist and even a bit hairy. (We humans tend to think the outsides of bodies are much prettier than the insides. This doll thought that, too.)

The other thing you would have noticed would be an explosion of coppery curls surrounding the freckles and the turned-up nose.

What would you do? What would you say? *What a sweet little girl? How nice of her to wake me? I certainly hope she'll be my friend?*

That might, indeed, be what you would say if you were an exceptionally kind doll . . . and exceptionally quick to gather your wits.

But if you were startled and bewildered and uncomfortably wet, you might be less than kind. And this doll was all those things. So she said instead, "Who's that big, ugly girl?"

After she said that, the doll heard footsteps pound across the room. Then she heard a door slam.

She paid no attention to the running and the slamming. She was too busy picking herself up and smoothing her gauzy pink dress. When her skirt was arranged to her satisfaction, she looked around.

That was better. She knew where she was now.

She was in her own bedroom. She could remember the bedroom. She especially remembered the dressing table. And she remembered the oval mirror. She sat down on the bench and gazed into the mirror.

She fluffed her golden hair. She touched her alabaster cheek.

(If you don't know that word—*alabaster*— it means smooth and white. At least that's what it means when it refers to cheeks.)

Then she said to the very pretty image smiling back at her, "I've almost forgotten. Who *are* you?"

The image didn't answer.

The doll touched the mirror with a delicate china finger.

The image reached out with an equally delicate finger to touch her.

The doll studied her golden hair, her blue

eyes, her alabaster cheeks. "You're utterly
perfect!" she said. "Surely you must be a
princess!"

Her image agreed by saying exactly the same
thing to her.

The doll reached up and formed a circle

with her hands above her golden hair. Yes, a crown was definitely called for.

"Of course," she said. And she nodded emphatically. Her image nodded, too. "A princess for sure."

Then she turned to look from her small dollhouse room to the larger one beyond. "I wonder," she said, "where my big, ugly servant ran off to."

As for the princess's "servant," shall we check on her now? The last time we heard about Zoey, she was slamming out of the bedroom.

Now she sat at the bottom of the stairs. The shock of the doll's sneeze had carried her that far. But once she'd reached the bottom step, she'd stopped, unable to go farther.

Too much had happened today. Too much was still happening.

Her mother and the grandmother she hadn't even known she had were still arguing in the kitchen. She could hear their voices, but by trying hard she could just manage to block out the words. Except for her name. From time to time one of them said "Zoey." She couldn't block that out.

Ordinarily Zoey might have listened in. In her situation you probably would, too. You would want to know what was wrong and what your mother and your grandmother were saying about you. But Zoey had too much on her mind to think about grown-ups' arguments.

She had the doll on her mind.

What she couldn't decide was whether to be thrilled or horribly hurt. A doll had actually sneezed. In her hand!

It had called her ugly.

No one had ever called her ugly before. She wasn't beautiful. Zoey knew that. Not in the way movie stars are beautiful. She had too many freckles. Her nose turned up too sharply. Her curls were too bushy and too red.

But her mother had freckles and bushy curls (though not red ones), and her mother wasn't ugly. So how could *she* be?

Anyway, just because a doll talked, did that mean you had to believe everything she said?

After a few moments, that very sensible question brought Zoey back to what mattered. She had found a doll. In her mother's old bedroom. The doll had sat up in her hand. She had sneezed!

Who cared what she said?

Zoey had been waiting her entire life for exactly such a thing to happen. And now, at last, it had.

And what had she done? She had run away!

All children who play with dolls like to pretend they walk and talk, of course. They feed them pretend meals. They take them to the doctor for shots.

But Zoey wasn't like other children. Not quite. She had never *pretended* her dolls walked and talked. Her entire life she had simply *known* they did. The problem was that, until now, she had never been able to catch one of them at it . . . the moving bit, that is.

At home in the apartment she shared with her mother, Zoey had three dolls—a baby doll, a Barbie, and a rag doll. She often lined this unlikely trio up on her bed. She'd position them carefully. The baby doll with a thumb in her mouth perhaps. Barbie standing with her head tilted just so. The rag doll with her legs crossed.

Then Zoey would say cheerfully, "I'm going to be gone all day, you know. I won't be back until dark. So have fun!" Or something like that so they would be fooled. And then she would march out, shut the bedroom door, and keep on walking, very loudly.

After a moment, though, she would tiptoe back and stand just on the other side of the door. And she would wait. She would wait as long as she could bear to, holding herself back and back and back. And when she couldn't wait another second, she'd throw the door open and spring into the room.

What she expected, every time, was to catch her dolls in different positions.

Maybe she would find the baby doll lying on her back, kicking her bare feet. Barbie would probably be sitting instead of standing, as Zoey had left her. Her head, instead of being tilted, would be perfectly straight. The rag doll might be doing back bends.

Always, though, they were too smart for her. Every single time she found them exactly as she'd left them. She could never figure out how they did it. How could they spring back into position so fast? But she'd never doubted what she knew . . . that they moved about the instant she left the room and that they managed to get back to the way they'd been just before she came in.

Being the kind of girl who believed such things, Zoey was probably less surprised to come across a sneezing, talking doll than you or I might be. Doing so just confirmed what she had always known.

She wasn't without feelings, though. And those feelings reminded her that she didn't like being called ugly.

"Well," she said at last. She smacked her hands against her knees and stood. "I guess I've got two choices. I can go see what Witch Hazel is brewing for lunch, or I can go back upstairs and give that rude doll a good talking-to."

And though she had named two choices and though she was, indeed, very hungry, she knew without question that only one choice was possible.

Zoey turned and climbed the stairs.

Chapter 4

A Name
for a Princess

The doll, in the meantime, was still sitting in front of the tiny mirror in her pink and white bedroom admiring herself. She was also sorting through names. What was she called before?

Adeline. Danielle. Lillian. Primrose.

Even as she sorted, though, she couldn't take her eyes off of the doll in the mirror.

Wasn't she gorgeous? Her china face was so lovely. Her hair so . . . golden!

Kaytlin. Vanessa. Wilhelmina.

What name would be right for a princess? And not just any princess, but one as perfect as she.

(I told you she was still admiring herself.)

She cocked her head. The mirror doll, of course, cocked her head, too.

She knew she'd had a name before she'd gone to sleep. Everyone has a name, after all. But she couldn't seem to remember what it was.

The problem was that waking always made her feel so muzzy! That's one of the few things she was certain of, besides that she was beautiful and a princess—waking *always* made her feel muzzy.

She tried to remember the before time, before she'd gone to sleep. But all she could call up was a succession of giant girls, one after another. Had they all been her servants? If she had always been a princess—and it was hard to imagine being anything else—then they must have been.

And speaking of servants, where had hers run off to, anyway? The doll turned from the mirror to check the larger room.

As if on cue, the big, ugly girl came through the door.

"Well," said the princess. She rose to face the girl, tiny fists bunched on her tiny hips. "Where have *you* been? Don't you know I need you?" And then, though she had spoken as firmly as a three-and-one-quarter-inch doll can, she found herself suddenly uncertain. What would the girl do? She remembered vaguely that these giant creatures could be unpredictable.

What she didn't know was that she had just spoken the magic words, *I need you.* (Zoey's mother said those words from time to time, *I need you.* And when she said them, it meant everything was fine. It meant that she wanted Zoey close.)

But the doll didn't know that. She didn't even know that Zoey was Zoey. That is, she didn't yet know her name. She did understand the smile that spread across Zoey's face, however. And she could see that, though the giant girl had come in clearly set for a fight, the fight had drained out of her in an instant.

"You need me?" the girl said. And she pressed both hands against her chest as though to make sure she was the *me* under discussion.

"Certainly," the doll said, "you're my . . ."

She stopped herself. She had almost said *owner,* but she didn't like that word. She had never liked it.

So she started over and said instead, "You're my servant, aren't you?"

"Am I?" the girl asked. And as if she had already answered her own question, she settled obediently onto the floor in front of the doll-house. She peered in at the doll, her face bright with questions.

The doll took a step back. She couldn't help it. She never quite got used to the size of these girls!

(Just imagine looking into a face, a very close face, twice as tall as you!)

Still, she knew it was important to take charge right from the beginning. So she put on her most royal tone. "Every princess has a servant," she said. "That means you're mine."

The girl's mouth dropped open. What a cavern her mouth was. Worse than her nose! The doll took another step back. She bumped into the canopied bed and sat down.

"Princess?" the girl said. "Are you really a princess?"

"Of course," the doll replied. "Can't you tell?" And though she spoke with assurance— a great deal of assurance for such a small doll— she felt uneasy. Why should this enormous girl believe her? If the creature wanted to, she could snatch her up again. Or simply squash her with a gigantic thumb.

The girl leaned even closer. The princess couldn't help herself. She shut her eyes.

When she opened them, the huge face was pressed so close to the open side of the dollhouse that the princess could have reached out and touched the turned-up nose. She didn't, though. She still wasn't feeling entirely friendly toward that nose.

"Is that why you're allowed to talk to me?" the face asked. "Because you're a princess and I'm your servant?"

Allowed. The doll didn't like that word any more than she liked *owner.* She didn't want to think that anyone *allowed* her anything. She talked to whomever she chose, didn't she?

Still, the idea of having a servant was good. Very good. Every princess needs a servant. So the doll turned things around just a bit when she replied. "That's it exactly," she said. "It's because you're my servant that you're allowed to hear me talk."

"Oh-h-h-h!" the girl said. The word came out long and slow, carried by a breath that was, for the tiny doll, like a warm wind blowing. Then the girl added, "But if I'm going to be your servant, I need to know your name. 'Princess . . .'?"

So here the doll was, right back where she'd started . . . trying to remember her own name. It wasn't her fault she couldn't remember, though. She assured herself of that. After all, what kind of a servant couldn't manage a simple task like keeping your name for you while you slept?

The doll drew herself up to her full three and one-quarter inches. "That's your job," she said. "Have you forgotten? You're supposed to keep my name in your mind every minute."

The girl's expression melted into worry.

The princess leaned into the worry. "When I wake, you're supposed to say, 'Welcome, Princess . . .' And then you use my name, you see?"

"I see." The girl nodded. She closed her eyes. The doll could practically see names scrolling across her freckled eyelids. When she opened them again, she said, "I don't suppose you'd like to be called Molly. Princess Molly? My best friend is named Molly."

"Of course not," the doll snapped. "No princess in the entire world has ever been named Molly."

The girl didn't argue. She just closed her eyes again. Her eyes, the doll noted before they closed, were a coppery color, as bright as her hair.

After a moment, the girl opened them once more. "Jessica? Ashley? Megan?"

"Ordinary." The doll shook her head. "My name isn't anything so ordinary."

"Amy?" the girl offered. But she said it in a way that already accepted the fact that Amy wasn't right, either.

This time the doll didn't bother to respond. Couldn't this creature come up with anything better than Jessica, Megan . . . Amy?

But even as she was thinking this, even as she was trying hard to remember her name herself, a voice floated up the stairs. "Zoey?" it called. "Are you up there?"

So that was this one's name . . . Zoey.

"Yes," Zoey answered the voice. "I'm here. I'm in your room."

Footsteps on the stairs. The doll went still. She didn't want this adult, whoever she was, to know that she had awakened. Nothing good ever came from a grown-up's discovering such a thing. They tended to get much too excited.

But the footsteps stopped, halfway up the stairs. "Hazel has fixed us some lunch," the voice called. "Come on down. Let's eat."

"I'll be right there, Mom," Zoey replied.

Clearly an obedient child, she stood immediately and started for the door. Then she stopped and turned around. "Do you want to come down and eat with me?" she asked.

"Of course not!" the doll replied, indignant. "Do you think I eat and drink like an ordinary human being?"

Zoey looked surprised, but then she said, "Eating is . . . well, it's kind of nice." She seemed almost hurt.

"Don't you know?" the doll said, trying to be patient. Sometimes these girls could be a bit slow. "If you eat, then you have to go to the bathroom. And that's disgusting!"

Zoey laughed, as if going to the bathroom were the funniest thing she'd ever heard of. "Okay, no lunch for you," she agreed. "But do you want to come downstairs anyway? You could watch *me* eat."

The doll thought about that. Those enormous teeth chomping. That cavernous mouth slurping. She shuddered.

But then she thought about being alone in the room again. That was even less appealing. She had been alone too long. Much too long. Loneliness had seeped inside her . . . (I almost said *inside her bones,* as if a tiny china doll had bones, which, of course, it doesn't.) But it had seeped inside every part of her until everything about her felt lonely, even her blue eyes and her alabaster skin. (And I know you remember that word, *alabaster.*)

So she said, "Well . . . since it's important to you, I'll come. But you have to remember the secret."

The girl was reaching to pick her up. "Secret?" she said, her hand suspended in the air. "What secret?"

"Grown-ups can never know."

"That you can walk and talk?"

"Of course," the doll said.

The girl nodded wisely. Apparently that was something she understood. Then she cupped the doll gently in her hand and lifted her into the air.

After the first rush the doll always felt when she was picked up, she settled comfortably into the curve of Zoey's fingers. She was ready, she told herself . . . for anything, for everything.

My, but it was good to be awake again!

Chapter 5

The Throne Room

Do you know what I mean when I say that an argument can change the air in a room, even after all the talking has stopped? When Zoey walked into the kitchen, the air felt heavy.

Neither her grandmother nor her mother spoke.

Hazel stood, leaning against the stove, her plump arms crossed.

Zoey's mother sat at the table, her spine curved into a question mark. She was concentrating on a bowl of tomato soup and a sandwich.

Another bowl of soup and another sand-wich, toasted golden brown and cut into two neat triangles, waited on the other side of the table. Zoey could see the cheese, all warm and gooey, oozing from the toasted bread.

She sat down in front of the food.

"I'm glad you're here, Zoey," Hazel said. She seemed to mean it.

Zoey smiled at her grandmother. She was glad, too, of course. Or at least she would have been glad if Hazel and her mother weren't arguing. Why were they so angry with one another, anyway?

Zoey peeked at the tiny doll cupped in her hand. She had gone rigid, as though she had never moved in her life, so Zoey figured it was safe to set her down. She propped her care-fully on the edge of her plate. She just fit there, her tiny feet resting on the table.

"I see you've found Regina," Hazel said. Her eyes were fastened on the doll.

"*Princess* Regina," Zoey's mother corrected, her voice sharp.

"*Princess* Regina," Hazel agreed, still studying the doll intently. Did she expect her to move? Zoey wondered. But then Hazel turned her gaze back to Zoey. "Your mother always insisted that Regina was a princess," she said.

Zoey nodded, satisfied. So that was the doll's name!

Princess Regina sat staring straight ahead, but Zoey could see that her tiny mouth had turned up at the corners. She was sure the doll hadn't been smiling before, at least not that much.

A light breeze wafting in the window over the sink gathered up the rich smell of tomato soup and toasted bread and stirred it around the room.

Zoey took a spoonful of soup. The warmth

of it followed all the way down to her stomach. She bit a point off one triangle of her sandwich and let the cheese melt on her tongue.

"Mom, did you used to play with Regina?" she asked, testing the name. "With *Princess* Regina?"

"Sure," her mother said. "Your grandmother

did, too. And her mother before her. I suppose her mother before that, too. Princess Regina has ruled this family for a long time."

"When we weren't being ruled by pure obstinacy," Zoey's grandmother said.

Zoey wasn't quite sure what "pure obstinacy" was, but judging by the look on her mother's face, this was the beginning of more arguing. She didn't want to hear it.

"It's kind of hot for soup today," she said, grabbing her sandwich in one hand and the doll in the other. "I think I'll take Princess Regina outside."

And without waiting for permission, either her mother's or her grandmother's, she rose from the table and headed for the front door.

"Be good," they both called after her.

Zoey ignored the command, whatever it meant. It was something grown-ups seemed to need to say—"Be good! Be good!"—as though, if they didn't say it at every turn, kids would go right out and rob a bank.

She let the slam of the screen door answer "Be good."

As soon as they were out of sight of the adults, the doll began to squirm in Zoey's hand. And the instant Zoey felt the movement, her irritation fell away.

A princess! A tiny princess! Of course she would be good! She would be too busy taking care of Princess Regina to be anything else.

Zoey took another bite of her sandwich and held Princess Regina up to inspect her. The afternoon sun glinted in the doll's golden hair.

"You're beautiful," Zoey said.

"I know," the princess replied. Somehow it didn't sound stuck-up when she said it, just matter-of-fact.

Zoey laughed. "Where do you want to go?" she asked. "You've lived here for . . . what? A hundred years? You must know all the best places."

"Of course I do," Princess Regina said. "We'll go to my throne room. Where else?"

"Okay," Zoey agreed easily enough. Then she waited. When the doll said nothing further, she asked, "Where is it?"

"You don't know where my throne room is?" Princess Regina exclaimed.

Zoey shrugged. "I don't know where any-thing is. I'm new here. I need you to show me."

Princess Regina threw up her tiny hands. "How can I show you? It's far away. Far, far away. It would take me a hundred years to walk there by myself."

Zoey considered that. If she put this tiny doll down in the grass, it would take her a hundred years to get almost anywhere. She couldn't even climb the steps to the porch to get back into the house!

"You're my servant," Princess Regina added, rather ominously. "It's your job to take me there."

Zoey sat down on the top step of the porch, set the doll on her knee, and took a big bite of her sandwich. "Maybe," she said around a mouthful of bread and cheese, "if you'll tell me what your throne room looks like, it will be easier for me to find."

And so the little doll did. In a dreamy voice, she talked and talked and talked.

Her throne room, she explained, was made of sunlight and shadows. It was made of lace . . . green lace. (*Not pink?* Zoey thought, but she didn't interrupt.) It was made of summer breezes and flowers. Every kind of flower.

The carpet was so soft that you didn't need

furniture. You could simply sink into it the way you would sink into a comfortable bed.

In fact, the only piece of furniture in the entire room was her throne. It was tall, tall enough that she could look out over everything. And it was covered with silvery-green velvet.

Her throne room was private, too. Nobody came there, nobody even knew about it except Princess Regina and whatever girl was her servant at the time.

Which means, Zoey thought, *I could go back inside and ask my mom and Hazel where the throne room is.* It probably wouldn't do any good, though. Grown-ups didn't seem to remember such things.

She didn't want to go back to the kitchen with its heavy air, anyway. So she picked up the doll and looked around. If she set her mind to it, she could find a place as wonderful as that.

Sunlight and shadows. Green lace. Soft carpet.

Her eyes scanned the front yard and the gravel road. She walked around the side of the house. The backyard went on and on, edged by the lilacs she had noticed before. And just beyond the lilacs lay woods. Deep woods.

Sunlight and shadows?

Was Princess Regina's "throne room" in the woods?

If it was, how would she ever find it?

Zoey was a city girl. She hadn't spent much time in the country. Such a large collection of trees didn't appeal to her at all. They looked forbidding. Once her Girl Scout troop had gone camping in a state park. The main thing she remembered from that was mosquitoes . . . and how dark it had been in the woods!

What would she do if Regina's throne room was hidden among the trees?

Then she saw something that made the skin along her arms tingle. In the back corner of the yard, just at the edge of the woods, but not in it, stood an enormous weeping willow tree. It rose and rose and rose, then each branch stretched out wide and bent back down to the grass. The leafy branches cascading to the ground looked exactly like green lace!

Zoey popped the last of her sandwich into her mouth, wiped the buttery crumbs on her shorts, and headed for the weeping willow.

When she stepped between the delicate branches into the hushed silence beneath the tree, she didn't even have to ask Princess Regina if she had the right place. She knew she did. There had never been a more perfect throne room!

"Finally," the little doll said, as though

Zoey had been extremely slow getting there, instead of walking right to it the way she had. "Now . . . you can put me on my throne."

It didn't take Zoey long to pick out the throne, either. At the base of the trunk was a large mossy rock. The top of the rock was indented, forming a velvety seat. At least it formed a seat for a very small doll.

Zoey set Princess Regina down carefully on the rock. Clearly she had guessed right, because the doll settled right in and pointed a royal finger. "Flowers," she commanded. "Go gather flowers."

Relieved to have gotten the first part right, Zoey curtsied obediently.

"Yes, Your Majesty," she said, and she went off in search of flowers.

Chapter 6

Princess and Servant

You may be wondering right about now why Zoey is so willing to obey a doll, especially one who stands only three and one-quarter inches tall. Surely not because she is afraid of such a tiny thing. Not because she has no mind of her own, either.

There is a reason, to be sure, and it comes out of something I haven't yet told you about Zoey.

Actually, there are many things I haven't told you about Zoey, about her mother . . . about everybody in this story. Lives are complicated things, you see, and the storyteller's task, as much as any other, is to make them appear simple and easy to understand. In order to do that, I choose. I choose what to tell you, when to tell it, and what to leave out. It is the nature of stories to leave out far more than they include.

For instance, I could have told you that Zoey's favorite color isn't really pink, it's purple. She used to like pink when she was a little girl, but now she prefers purple. And her mother has never noticed that she has grown beyond pink to purple. That's just the way her mother is. She loves every inch of Zoey, but her mind is very . . . well, perhaps the best word is *full*. Her mind is so full, in fact, that she often doesn't notice things like Zoey's growing from pink to purple.

But Zoey's favorite color isn't part of this

story. Not really. So let's talk about something that is.

For as long as Zoey can remember, she and her mother have had a favorite game. They call it Princess and Servant. One pretends to be a princess and orders the other about. For instance, the princess says, "Go find me a sip of nectar so sweet it will curl my toes." And the servant comes back with a thimble full of the brine from the jar of sweet pickles in the refrigerator. Then they turn the game around, and the other one is the princess for a time, asking, perhaps, for a puff of wind.

As you can guess, Zoey's mother learned the game from Princess Regina. What she didn't learn from Regina, though, was changing the roles about. The doll, as I'll bet you can also guess, *never* in her long existence has played the servant.

Anyway, Zoey has always loved playing Princess and Servant with her mother. So when Regina announced that she was a princess and that Zoey was her servant, Zoey fell in with the idea happily. Perhaps the time will come when Zoey will decide that she has plans for her life beyond being a servant to a tiny doll. But that isn't going to happen just yet.

So let's look at what *is* going to happen.

The last time we saw Princess Regina, she was sitting high on her mossy throne. And that's where we'll find her still, on her throne, gazing about.

Ah, she is thinking, *how fine it is to be awake and a princess!*

How fine it was, also, to have her servant off gathering flowers for her. She *loved* flowers! They grew, she was certain, especially for her.

She also loved sitting on her throne,

watching the sunbeams play hide-and-seek among the dancing leaves.

But best of all, she loved being in charge once more. Nothing could be better than being a princess and awake and in charge!

Regina smoothed her gauzy pink dress.

This particular giant girl made an especially obedient servant. Princess Regina was glad about that. Some of the servants she'd had in the past had not always been quite so willing.

Regina frowned and shook her head thinking about those girls.

But then she looked about again and smiled once more.

At the dancing leaves.

At the glimmering sunlight.

At her mossy throne.

Silence wrapped her like a comforting quilt.

At least the silence would have been

comforting if she hadn't been growing a bit uneasy.

A light breeze riffled the lacy walls of her throne room, making only the faintest whisper. A disagreeably large bee bumbled by. It buzzed in front of Regina's face for an instant. Then, realizing its mistake, it moved on.

Leaving Regina alone.

Entirely alone.

She squirmed on her throne. Surely her

servant didn't need to take so long at her task!

What was this giant girl's name, anyway? *Oh . . . that's right. Zoey.*

Zoey should have been back by now.

When the girl did come back, she was going to get a good scolding for being gone so long. Not a severe one. Regina didn't want to see more of those messy tears. But she would certainly be firm.

After all, why should anyone need this much time just to gather a few flowers?

Unless . . .

Unless . . .

Unless she didn't intend to come back!

Regina frowned again and tried to peer through the wall of leaves.

Where was Zoey, anyway? How could she be so thoughtless as to go off and leave her for so long?

So thoughtless and so cruel.

Now, you and I know Zoey. We know perfectly well that she would never go off and leave a doll that had just sneezed in her hand. If she is taking a long time—and she is—it's because she wants to do an exceptional job of pleasing the princess. Or because something else has called her away for a time. Or both.

But Princess Regina didn't yet know Zoey as well as we do. And besides, she had her own reasons for suspicion.

She remembered another giant girl.

Her name was Rose, and one of the things the princess remembered about Rose was that she was a fantastic playmate.

She carried Regina with her everywhere, and together they always had the finest adventures. Rose climbed trees and waded in the creek in the woods and spun her bicycle in the gravel road. She danced to any music that floated by on the air, and once, under a full moon, she even slipped out of her bedroom window and scooted down the rose trellis to dance in the silent moonlight.

Rose had been more fun than any girl the little doll had ever known, and most of the time she kept the tiny doll close . . . in a pocket or tied on a ribbon around her neck, or sometimes just cupped in her hand.

Except that sometimes—Princess Regina never quite understood how it happened— sometimes, Rose forgot. About Princess Regina, that is.

And when she forgot, she simply disappeared. Vanished!

So that Princess Regina would find herself in the crack between the couch cushions, or on the damp basement floor, or even sitting on a clod of dirt in the garden . . . alone.

Once the princess sat on her mossy throne beneath the weeping willow tree and watched the light fade in the lacy leaves. She watched the dark gobble up everything, the leaves, her mossy throne, even her own hands clenched in her lap.

When such a thing happened, Princess Regina became angry. Utterly furious. Then she grew frightened.

And then she went still.

First she'd feel alone in the world. And then she would feel nothing at all . . . until she found herself again in the hands of a giant girl, a giant *weeping* girl.

Princess Regina had never understood why being able to move and see and hear sometimes slipped away from her or what made her come awake again. But she was sure of one thing—

when she was left alone for too long, it happened.

Her breath would begin to come in short gasps.

The way it was coming now.

Her arms and legs would tingle.

Just as they were tingling now.

Her whole body would start to feel heavy. So heavy she could barely move it.

And then . . . and then . . .

"Zoey!" Regina called. Or she tried to call, but no sound—not even a tiny one—came from her mouth.

She could no longer blink, no longer move, no longer form a thought. Not even a frightened one. Nor even an angry one.

And then the princess was a doll again. Only that. A tiny doll made of fine china.

Beautiful, but completely still.

Zoey, of course, knew nothing about what was happening to Princess Regina. She was too busy gathering flowers.

And then she'd had to go back inside the house. She made herself go in to ask if she could pick an iris—just one—from Hazel's

garden. She had found lots of flowers, but one of the majestic purple irises growing by the back door was exactly what a bouquet for a princess needed.

"Yes," Hazel had said when Zoey asked. "Of course." And before Zoey could thank her and go on her way again, she'd added, "Would you like some ice cream?" Homemade vanilla ice cream in a bright blue bowl, with chocolate sauce poured over it and peanuts crumbled on top. (The argument had stopped, at least for the moment, when Zoey came into the kitchen.)

Zoey would have run back to the weeping willow tree to get Princess Regina before she sat down to the ice cream, but since the doll didn't eat—*couldn't* eat, apparently— there seemed no point. Besides, Princess Regina might feel bad, sitting there next to ice cream she couldn't even taste.

All of which meant that Zoey had been gone longer than she had meant to be when, at last, she burst through the delicate branches of the weeping willow, her hands stuffed to overflowing with flowers.

"Look! Just look what I found!" she cried, and she held out her bouquet.

She'd found a few lilacs that were still fresh. At the edge of the woods, she'd picked some white flowers and some pink ones, too. She didn't know what they were called, but she would find out their names later. Hazel would know their names, she was sure, but she hadn't wanted to go back in again to ask.

She'd added bright yellow dandelions to the bouquet, too. There were lots of bright yellow dandelions growing in her grandmother's yard.

And there was, of course, the one perfect iris she had picked, with permission, from

Hazel's flower garden by the back door.

"Look!" Zoey cried again. "Flowers for Your Royal Highness!" That's the way she and her mother talked when they played the game. "Your Royal Highness." "Your Majesty." Sometimes even silly, made-up titles like "Your High Royalness."

Zoey knelt in front of the mossy throne and spread her bouquet out on the ground before Princess Regina. Then she checked the tiny doll's face. Was she pleased?

Zoey looked. Then she looked again, harder.

"Princess Regina?" she said. And she reached out a careful finger to touch the doll's arm.

But Princess Regina didn't answer. And she didn't move. And her arm . . . there was something wrong with her arm. It felt hard, of course. It always felt hard. After all, Princess Regina was made out of china.

Now it felt still.

Too still.

"Princess?" Zoey touched the doll's other arm.

Nothing.

"Princess Regina?" She stroked the doll's face.

More nothing.

And then—I'm sure you'll understand, Zoey wasn't a crybaby by any means, but she couldn't help it—she snatched up the silent doll and burst into tears.

Chapter 7

The Secret

Zoey ran for the house. Where else could she go? As she ran, she sobbed and, with both hands, swiped at the tears running down her cheeks.

One hand held the tiny doll, so Regina's golden hair and gauzy pink dress were soon soaked.

As Zoey approached the front porch, though, she slowed. When she came to the bottom of the steps, she stopped.

What was it that Princess Regina had said to her? *Grown-ups can never know.*

If she ran to her mother and Hazel, she would have to tell them why she was crying. And if she told them why, she would be giving away the secret.

And if she gave away Princess Regina's secret, the doll would be taken away from her. She was sure of it. Grown-ups never let you keep anything really good.

Even if her mother and grandmother didn't behave like other grown-ups and take the doll away, the magic would probably be destroyed if they knew. Princess Regina might never walk and talk again.

Zoey plopped down on the bottom step and held the tiny doll out in front of her. "What happened?" she pleaded. "Why did you go away?"

And Princess Regina, who had without question been silent and unmoving when Zoey had found her on the throne beneath the weeping willow tree, answered in a shrill voice, "Away? What do you mean, away? You're the one who went away!"

"I . . . I . . ." The accusation was so absurd that Zoey didn't know how to defend herself. She had done what the princess had told her to do. That was all. She had gone to gather flowers, and she hadn't taken all that long, either!

Well . . . maybe a little bit long. Picking the dandelions had probably slowed her down some. And then, of course, there was the ice cream. You couldn't eat ice cream too fast or you'd get an ice cream headache. And it was too good to eat really fast, anyway.

But still . . .

"And now," the princess went on, "look what you've done to my dress. Look what you've done to me!" She pushed at Zoey's fingers as though she thought she could stand in the air if Zoey would only let go. "You've smeared your messy tears all over me."

Zoey had no answer to that. It was true. Princess Regina *was* wet all over. Her gauzy pink dress was damp and wrinkled. Her golden hair was darkened with moisture. Even her face glistened with Zoey's tears.

Zoey was sorry to have gotten the doll wet. She truly was. But still . . . Princess Regina *was* awake again! That was what mattered. She was completely, even obnoxiously, awake. And Zoey couldn't have been more delighted. She was so happy, in fact, that she hardly minded being yelled at!

"I'm sorry," she said. "I'm really sorry. I didn't mean to get you wet. But I'm so glad you're— OUCH!"

Zoey barely stopped herself from dropping

the tiny doll. "Did you bite me?" she cried. She changed Princess Regina to the other hand and shook the hand that had been holding her. "Did you really bite me?"

It hadn't been a serious bite, to be sure. The doll's mouth was too small to do much damage. But it had definitely been a bite.

"Take me back to my room!" Princess Regina ordered, not bothering to answer the question. "I want to go to my room this very minute!"

That was easy enough to do, so Zoey slipped back inside the house and up the stairs. (She cocked an ear toward the kitchen as she did. The cross voices had started up again, climbing over and over one another.)

When Zoey reached the bedroom, she shut the door to keep out the noise.

"Put me down!" the princess ordered.

Zoey set her down carefully on the bed in
the dollhouse. "I . . . I'm glad you're awake
again," she said.

"I'm always awake!" the tiny doll snapped.
"What are you accusing me of, anyway?"

Zoey didn't know how to answer that. She hadn't meant to *accuse* Regina of anything. But clearly the tiny doll hadn't been awake when Zoey had come back with the flowers. Was there nothing she could say without offending Her Royal Highness?

Her High Royalness, Zoey thought grumpily.

She sat down on the side of the bed, directly across from the dollhouse, and waited to see what would happen next.

The tiny doll kept swiping at her skin, shearing away Zoey's tears and grumbling under her breath. At last she spoke up. "You're just like *her*. You know that?" she said. "Just *like* her!"

"Like who?" Zoey asked, confused.

"She used to go off and leave me, too," the princess went on, again not answering Zoey's question. "She'd forget all about me.

And she wouldn't come back, either. The same as you!"

"I didn't forget—" Zoey started to say, but the doll interrupted.

"You don't know what it's like," she accused. Her voice was as brittle as glass. "How could you ever know what it's like to be alone in the world? Nobody to take care of you. Nobody who cares about you. Nobody at all!"

"I . . . I . . . ," Zoey said, but this time, though the princess didn't interrupt her, she stopped herself. In fact, her thought just snapped in two.

She truly didn't know what it was like to have no one to take care of her. Did she?

Somehow she couldn't seem to answer her own question.

But then the princess was talking again,

so Zoey pushed the terrible thought aside.

"Is it true?" the doll said. She sounded less angry now, even a bit uncertain. She looked away from Zoey and twisted the bottom of her skirt so that water dripped from it. "Just now . . . did I really go to sleep?"

Zoey wasn't sure she wanted to reply. The princess would probably yell at her again. But besides being a brave girl, which is something I've already told you, Zoey was also a truthful one. So she said, "You did. You were asleep when I came back with the flowers. And I couldn't wake you. I tried. Honest."

"So just for a minute there, I wasn't talking or moving or . . . anything?"

"You were as still as still," Zoey told her.

Princess Regina shuddered. She reached with both hands to touch her damp hair but then let her arms fall to her sides again.

"But now you're all right," Zoey assured her. "So it doesn't matter, does it? You're awake and—"

Once more the doll interrupted. "But *why* did it happen? *How* did it happen? What makes me go"—she shuddered again—"what makes me go to sleep?"

Zoey wanted very much to help, but she had no answer. If only she could ask her mother or her grandmother.

There was no point in asking them anything, though. All they cared about was yelling at one another. Remembering their angry voices made Zoey's stomach go tight.

Why were they so angry, anyway? And why did she keep hearing her name—*Zoey, Zoey*—again and again?

And why, for that matter, had her mother brought her here after all these years of not even mentioning that Zoey had a grandmother? Why had she asked Zoey to pack a suitcase but had packed nothing for herself? Not even a toothbrush!

And who was the little doll talking about when she said *she . . . she? She used to go off and leave me.*

Zoey found that she wanted to think about all that even less than she wanted to think about the argument going on in the kitchen.

She turned her attention instead to the doll's question. What made Princess Regina go to sleep?

Besides being a brave girl, and a truthful one, Zoey was a thoughtful one. And so she said, reaching deep into her own heart, "Is it maybe because you get lonely?"

Her reward for her well-intentioned words was a very cross look from the little doll.

And Princess Regina had reason to be cross. She hated, positively hated, this business of waking and discovering that she had been . . . gone. Who knew how much of the world slipped by while she was in such a state? Or what might happen to her while she couldn't see or hear or feel?

And what did *lonely* have to do with anything, anyway? She was a princess. Princesses didn't get lonely.

Regina scrubbed at her damp arm again and tried once more to wring out her hair.

And that was when it dawned on her.

The secret! Of course! It was water. It had to be water. Wasn't she wet every single time she woke up?

Hadn't Zoey been crying all over her the first time? Not a lot of tears, but at least one

big one. Then after she'd gone to sleep on her throne, hadn't Zoey blubbered all over her again? And wasn't that what happened every time? She'd open her eyes and there'd be an enormous face looming over her. A great salty tear would be splashing onto her face, running into her ears, soaking her hair.

And when she'd been away from whatever girl it was for too long, wasn't that when she slipped into sleep again?

Every time?

Surely that had been the secret all along—water! She should have thought of it before.

What a perfect answer!

Perfect, because water was something she could take charge of. All she had to do to stop going off to sleep was to keep water close by. She could rub it on herself whenever a girl went off and left her alone. She never had to let anyone weep all over her again.

Not this girl. Not any other girl.

Her plan formed, Princess Regina stood. "Bring me water!" she ordered in a loud voice. (Or at least the order came out as loud as a three-and-one-quarter-inch doll can muster.) "Immediately."

And, of course, since Zoey was used to providing for a princess, that's exactly what she did.

Zoey sat on the bed, watching. Regina dipped water from the paper cup Zoey had brought from the bathroom. She held it in her hand, then scrubbed her face. She dipped again and spread the water up and down her arm. Then she wet the other arm.

She even peeled off her pink dress. "Rinse this for me," she ordered, standing there in her bloomers and camisole. "I don't want your salty tears in my dress."

Zoey sighed, but she carried the tiny dress to the bathroom and held it under the faucet. She supposed it made sense, Regina's not wanting the salt of her tears in the dress or on her skin, but it was hard not to be a bit offended. The doll acted as though her tears were poison!

She squeezed the tiny dress out and rolled it in a towel to blot it. Then she carried it back to the bedroom.

"Do you want me to hang it up to dry?" she asked Regina.

But when she looked to Regina for an answer, she gasped.

The tiny doll had fallen over. Apparently she had grabbed the paper cup when she went

down, and that had tipped, too. Princess Regina, the rug on the dollhouse floor, everything, was soaked.

Much worse than the mess, though, was the princess herself. She lay in the puddle, as stiff and still as a . . . well, as any ordinary doll.

"Oh!" Zoey exclaimed. "Oh!" And she snatched up Regina and tried to dry her off with the bottom of her T-shirt.

But though Zoey's shirt made a pretty good towel, the doll remained rigid in her hand.

"Princess Regina!" Zoey cried.

The princess managed to get only one response past her stiffening lips. "Tears," she said. "It must have been the tears!"

And yet again, she went still in Zoey's hand.

Chapter 8

"Be Good."

Just about now, you're probably wondering what kind of story this is, anyway.

In most stories, if a doll can walk and talk, it stays that way. It doesn't keep blinking on and off again like a neon light. In fact, in most stories about dolls, no one even asks how a doll came to walk and talk. It just shows up that way at the beginning of the story and never changes.

So this story is, I suppose, a bit odd.

It may be odd in another way, too. I'll bet

in the stories you've read before, mothers were around for the usual reasons—to dispense cookies and sweaters and advice. But you didn't have to pay much attention to them. They were just *there*, part of the ground the story stood on.

The way our mothers are part of the ground we all stand on.

But Princess Regina wasn't like most dolls in stories, and Zoey's mother wasn't like most mothers, either in stories or out.

She was more fun, for one thing.

She was also a bit like the china doll. She blinked on and off again. The off times were harder for Zoey to think about than the on ones, though.

So mostly she didn't let herself think.

And she didn't let herself think now, either. Except about the doll.

The princess was doing this intentionally, all this going away. Zoey was certain she was. She just went off to sleep any time she pleased because she liked making people feel bad.

She was *that* kind of doll.

Zoey had heard what Regina said the last time she'd gone still. "It must have been the tears," she'd said. As though that's what she'd wanted . . . for Zoey to cry.

Well, it might be what the princess wanted, but that didn't mean she was going to get it.

Not *her* tears! Not one single drop more!

Zoey stuffed the tiny doll into the pocket of her shorts and hurried downstairs.

She would see if her mother and her grand-mother had finally stopped arguing. And if they hadn't . . . well, if they were still talking at one another in those angry voices, she would say something to get their attention. Maybe she'd tell them how much she hated listening to them, arguing and arguing the way they were.

But when Zoey burst into the kitchen, no argument was going on. In fact, nothing was going on at all.

The kitchen was bare and clean. Hazel stood alone at the sink, washing up the few dishes that had been used for their late lunch.

And Zoey's mother was nowhere to be seen.

Zoey stood very still in the doorway. "Where is she?" she asked. "Where did my mother go?" Her voice came out high and tight on the word *go,* almost as though she were going to cry, but, of course, she wasn't. She had no intention of crying.

Hazel looked over her plump shoulder at Zoey, but she didn't say anything. Zoey didn't wait for an answer, anyway. She turned and ran for the front door.

She stopped in the middle of the porch. What she saw was exactly what she had known she was going to see.

Her mother was there. She was out at the end of the stone walkway. She was opening the car door. She was getting in.

"Mom!" Zoey cried. And she was almost surprised when her mother turned back to look at her. She already had one foot inside the car, though, and she didn't take it out again.

"Oh," she said, "there you are!" As if she'd come to find Zoey, not the other way around. "I wanted to say good-bye."

"Good-bye?" Zoey echoed. "What do you mean? Where are you going?"

"Home," Zoey's mother said. She said it simply. She said it as though they had agreed about all this earlier . . . that she would go home and leave Zoey behind.

"No!" Zoey cried. She flew down the steps and along the stone walkway and grabbed her mother's arm. "You can't go. Not without *me*!"

But Zoey's mother shook her head. She had already started shaking her head even before Zoey spoke.

"I need to be by myself, Zoey," she said. Again she said it simply, flatly. As if it were something they both already knew.

And though Zoey had never heard the words before, it was true that her heart did know them. Her heart had known them since she was a tiny baby, lying in her mother's arms. That her mother would go away someday. That she would say, "I need to be by myself, Zoey," and she would go.

But already knowing the words in her heart didn't make them easier to hear.

"*You* need!" she cried. "*You* need! What about me? You're my mother. Don't you remember that you're my mother?"

Her mother nodded this time. Yes, she remembered. But even as she nodded, she was slipping behind the steering wheel, putting her key in the ignition.

Zoey clung to her mother's arm.

This wasn't happening! It couldn't be happening!

"You must understand, Zoey," her mother said. "I have to go." She said it with a finality that passed through Zoey like a blade.

And though it was the last thing in the world Zoey wanted to do, her hand let go of her mother's arm. It was as though her hand belonged to someone else, someone who agreed that her mother had to go.

Zoey's feet seemed to belong to that same someone. They stepped back from the car.

The car door shut. The motor rumbled to life. The window rolled down.

"Be good," her mother said, and Zoey wanted to block her ears against the mother-sounding words. *Be good.* As though she had ever been anything else!

Zoey's mother smiled, a quick, bright smile that flashed on, then off again. She backed the car out, turned, pulled away.

Then the dust roiled up behind the car like smoke.

And she was gone.

Zoey stood there for a long time, watching her world burn away.

At last, when there was nothing else to do, she turned back toward the empty house.

Almost empty. Hazel stood on the edge of the porch watching her. She held her arms out for Zoey.

Zoey knew her grandmother wanted her to come to her. Instead, she reached into the pocket of her shorts and took out the tiny china doll.

She threw Princess Regina at her grand-mother with all her might.

Chapter 9

A Kiss

It was a good thing Hazel was so soft. And a good thing she was quick, too. She caught the tiny doll against her stomach.

"I'm sorry, Zoey," she said. Once more she held out her arms. "I'm truly sorry."

But Zoey didn't move. "Will she come back?" she asked.

Hazel sighed. "I hope so," she said. "I've always hoped so." And then, when Zoey still didn't come to her, she added, "Until she does, we have one another." She held up the tiny doll. "And we have Princess Regina."

Without a word, Zoey walked past her grandmother and into the house.

Princess Regina woke with that familiar feeling. Wet. She wiped her face and sat up.

Where was she? Pale moonlight spread all around her, so she could see perfectly clearly, but still she didn't understand. . . .

Oh! She was on a pillow, and the giant girl—Zoey, that's right, this one was called Zoey—was blubbering all over her again.

Would she never stop?

But to tell the truth, Zoey wasn't really blubbering. She was sleeping. Perhaps she was dreaming. And a tear or two had simply slipped out, run down her cheek, and caught the tiny doll on their way to the pillow.

Zoey didn't even know Princess Regina was

next to her on the pillow. She had gone to bed alone, and after she was asleep, her grandmother had tiptoed in and laid the tiny doll next to her cheek.

"Take care of her," she had whispered, but I'm not sure whether she was asking the girl to take care of the doll or the doll to take care of the girl.

Both, maybe.

In any case, here Regina was, soggy with tears again . . . awake again.

All of which made her realize that she had been right in what she'd said as she was going off to sleep last time. Tears were the answer. It was tears that woke her up!

A messy solution, but an easy one. The only thing she had to do was to keep this enormous girl crying.

She reached up and wiped the dampness from Zoey's cheek and rubbed it into her throat.

How would she do it, though? She could hardly order Zoey to cry for her. As far as she could tell, people didn't cry on command like that. And she didn't want to have to depend on Zoey, anyway . . . or on anyone else.

And then—just like that—she had the answer. Regina didn't quite know how she knew, but she did. She knew exactly how she could keep Zoey's tears coming!

The princess stood on her tiptoes and whispered into the deep cave of the girl's ear. "Mother," she said. And instantly another tear came rolling toward her.

Regina gathered the moisture and rubbed it on the back of her neck, up and down her arms.

"Mother!" she whispered again.

She was rewarded with another tear.

"Mother!" she said, a bit more loudly.

Zoey's eyes flew open!

So, here we are. Princess Regina is awake once more. She's awake, but she has been caught milking Zoey for tears.

Zoey . . . well, Zoey is angry, and not only with the doll. After all, her mother has just driven right out of this story, leaving her behind with a stranger. It helps very little that the stranger is her grandmother.

Zoey sat up in bed and glared at the doll.

"I'm sorry!" Princess Regina said. She scooted backward until she came to the cliff at the edge of the bed.

"You're not sorry," Zoey said. "Not even *that* much." And she held her thumb and forefinger up with only a hair's-breadth of space between them to show how little she believed in *sorry*.

Princess Regina *was* sorry, though . . . truly. And not just sorry she'd been caught. (Everybody feels sorry about that.) For the first time in her long, on-and-off existence, she was looking out through her brilliant blue eyes and actually seeing.

Zoey's cheeks were flushed and her eyes snapped with anger, but behind the snap lay loss so deep that the tiny doll thought she might drown in it.

"She's left you before, hasn't she?" Regina spoke softly, but her words rang like an iron gong. "She's left you lots of times."

"My mother?" Zoey cried. "Are you talking about my mother? Never! She's never left me!"

"Never?" Regina said.

"Not ever!" Zoey insisted. But then, maybe because she absolutely, under no circumstances was going to please this doll by crying again, words began tumbling out instead. "Sometimes she stays in bed," she told her. "That's all. Sometimes she gets so tired she can't get up, and then she stays in bed. But she doesn't *leave* me."

"And what do you do when your mother stays in bed?" Regina asked, still in that soft-iron voice. "Who takes care of you?"

Zoey shook her head from side to side as though she were trying to shake away flies buzzing at her. But she answered anyway. "There used to be a neighbor from across the hall," she said. "Her name was Mrs. Lane. She'd come get me when she heard . . ."

She stopped.

"When she heard what?" the doll asked.

"When she heard me cry," Zoey answered, her chin thrust out like a battering ram. "I was little, so I used to cry. But I don't do that anymore. Besides, Mrs. Lane moved away, so now I take care of myself."

"You really do? You take care of yourself?" Princess Regina couldn't help but be impressed. For all of her long life, despite her independence, she knew there was little she could do without one or the other of these enormous girls. Why, she couldn't even reach her throne room by herself!

"I get myself dressed for school," Zoey told her. "I wash my face and brush my hair. And I eat Cheerios from the box. I like Cheerios best that way, anyway. When Mama's there, she makes me eat them with milk."

Regina had never eaten, not Cheerios or anything else, but somehow she understood the difference between cereal straight from the box and cereal with milk. Even if you liked it straight from the box, you wanted your mother to insist on milk.

Princess Regina was beginning to understand many things.

"Your mother's name is Rose," she said. It was a statement rather than a question.

Tears brimmed, then tumbled down Zoey's cheeks.

You might expect that the little doll would have rushed to catch the life-giving moisture. After all, now she knew how much she needed it.

But she didn't. The understanding that was dawning was so huge, so heavy, that the weight of it made her sit down hard on the pillow.

This girl—this brave, lonely girl—was just like her. She, too, could be frightened . . . and angry . . . and lost. She could even go still inside!

Princess Regina reached up to touch her own eyes. For some strange reason they were stinging.

Her eyes had always *seen* perfectly well. At least they saw everything she wanted to see when she was awake. They had seen sunshine and pink and her own image in a mirror. They had shut against giant faces thrust too close to hers. But this was the first time they had ever stung like this.

And it was certainly the first time her own eyes had ever made tears.

"Oh!" Princess Regina said.

And Zoey said "Oh!" too.

Because, as the tears fell, the most amazing transformation was taking place. The perfect china doll was suddenly . . . well, less than perfect. A little freckle appeared here, a tiny mole there. Her golden hair dulled, just a bit. One fingernail actually seemed to be a bit jagged.

But beneath the tears, her vivid blue eyes sparked with life.

"I . . . I'm *soft*," Regina said, holding up a tiny arm. "My skin is soft!"

"You're alive," Zoey said, lifting the doll in the palm of her hand and wiping away the minuscule tears with her thumb. "You've cried, and now you're alive!"

And then, completely forgetting her proper role as servant, Zoey gave the princess a tender kiss.

To the princess's own surprise, she kissed Zoey back.

Chapter 10

"Not Today, I Think."

So . . . where does this story end?

With Zoey's mother coming back?

I wish I could tell you that was so, but though she may come back someday, that hasn't happened yet.

With Zoey and Regina becoming good, good friends?

Yes. That one's right.

With Princess Regina learning how to eat?

That's right, too. Her favorite foods are tiny

peas, fresh from Hazel's garden, and the crispy tip of the wing from a roasted chicken.

And ice cream, of course.

She thinks a person might as well eat tree bark as try to chew celery, but that may be only because her teeth are so small.

And, naturally, she's had to learn about going to the bathroom, too.

At first Zoey thought she was going to have to put the doll in tiny diapers, because Regina didn't pay that much attention to what was going on down there. The princess didn't like being messy, though, so she learned pretty fast.

She's had something else to learn, too . . . that flesh is exceedingly tender. A china doll can break, but skin can bruise and bleed.

It can sing when it is stroked, too.

"Does being made of blood and bones mean

that I will die?" Regina asked suddenly one bright blue morning.

Taken by surprise, Zoey looked to her grandmother. And Hazel, wise and loving Hazel, answered. (It turned out she had not forgotten nearly as much as the doll and the girl had thought.)

"Not today, I think" is what she said.

So Zoey and Princess Regina have learned to live with that. *Not today.* Not today for dying, or for Zoey's mother coming back, either.

But today for waking, for being delighted to see one another, for dipping a corner of toast—or a crumb—into the runny yolk of a fried egg.

For smelling the good, dark smell of the earth.

Today for making up games in the throne room, too.

Princess Regina still doesn't care much for changing the roles about, but she tries it now and then, just the same.

Together they have learned that today, every day, is a day to be brave in, a day to be alive in . . . a day to love in.

And if a few tears fall? Well, a good friend can always be counted on to wipe them away.

Isn't that so?